Who Said That???

By

Gill Burnett

Other Books by Gill Burnett

Take Note
Note Taken
Last Note

Cushie Butterfield
Mack Book
Show Me a Sign!!

By Gill Burnett & Freddie Jones

Eddie the Elf

Copyright © Gill Burnett 2023
This book is sold subject to the condition that it shall not, by way of trade or otherwise, be lent, resold, hired out, or otherwise circulated without the publisher's prior consent in any form of binding or cover other than that in which it is published and without similar condition including this condition being imposed on the subsequent publisher.
The moral right of Gill Burnett has been asserted.

Foreword

Hi, im Freddie (Gills grandson) and after writing Eddie the Elf with my Marmar I decided that I wanted her to write another children's book, but this time more grown up. Walking through the streets of Burnopfield talking about reincarnation, I came up with the idea that I wanted to write a book, all about a famous dead person living in someone's head. After time went on, we came up with a plan, and had the original name of Freddie Mercury. Time had passed and we were left a lonely half-finished book, that we really didn't know what to do with. Now, it is finished, and has been published for you to buy. Hope you have a great day!

Love Freddie xxx

Aged 10

Chapter 1

Billy Watson turned 14 years old the day that the United Kingdom went into a National Lockdown with the arrival of the Covid 19 Pandemic.

The lockdown changed Billy's life forever. Like everyone else, the Covid Pandemic came along and for months and months, people lived scared. No one knew what the virus was all about, but they all saw the images on the television, and all watched on as people lost their lives because the doctors and nurses had no idea how to treat this alien infection.

Normal life stopped. There was no going to school or going to work and in Billy's house, their usual pristine conservatory became a makeshift office with an ever-ringing telephone and machines that whirled and chugged from dawn until dusk.

Billy's mam and dad ran their own small decorating company, employed about 10 people. But overnight, the work had all had to stop and with no idea when they would be allowed to start working again, it became a daily routine for both his mam and dad to be on the telephone to customers trying to sort out new dates and speaking to their employees trying to sort wages. All of this was usually done with his mam in her pyjamas and his dad in shorts, t shirts and both of them wearing their slippers.

It was the strangest of times.

For Billy there was no school, no football training, no piano lessons, and no friends. Beyond the walls of their home, there was nothing.

Their house had always been full of hustle and bustle. His friends, his older sister Emily and her friends and her boyfriend and her boyfriend's

friends. Then there were the people who worked for his mam and dad and on top of that there were all of the relatives.

The people Billy missed most were his Grandmas and Granddads. They were always over, because his mam and dad ran their own business they were often at work, Grandmas and Granadas helped out with the childcare. Sometimes it would be one Grandma, or one Grandma and one Granddad, or two Grandmas or two Granddads, whatever was needed and who ever could do it and they would be there.

And then they were not.

They would ring up on the telephone every day and even though they were old they were all very good at texting and when it looked like lockdown was a way of life for a long time, they managed to set up their laptops so they could have Zoom calls. It was a different type of family life.

Billy and his family did all the Grandmas and Granddads shopping. Twice a week the grocery van would come to their house and there was enough food delivered to feed the street, not just three families. It would be divided out and then Billy and his mam or his dad would deliver it to the Grandmas and Grandads houses.

They would run up the path, dump the shopping on the doorstep and then run away to stand at the edge of the garden to wave and shout to each other. That went on for months.

The novelty of not being at school soon wore off. In the beginning he liked just sitting around playing on his computer games. Going to bed late and getting up even later, there was just nothing to get him out of bed for. But even that got boring. He watched every box set and movie that he could find on television and even read the books that he had been set by his English teacher at the beginning of term, something he would normally struggle to do. He would normally never have the time.

When one of the Granddads told him that he had sorted him a box of DVDs out for him to watch, Billy really had not been hopeful. Billy liked science fiction and Marvel; something that he had never heard his Granddad say he liked. But on shopping delivery day, there was a box jam packed with DVDs on the step waiting for him, there would surely be some that Billy would enjoy!!

When he got home, Billy took the box straight up to his bedroom and then realised that he had nothing to play a DVD on! Everything he watched was streamed. His new laptop did not even have a CD facility. It took hours dismantling the garage to find a DVD player and then further hours looking for all of the suitable leads in a bag full of leads which had somehow managed to tie themselves all together in the plastic carrier bag. Billy did not mind; time was something he seemed to have plenty of.

And then happy that he had everything set up just so, he began.

None of the pictures on the DVDs appealed to him, and the blurbs were vague, so he started at the first one and began to make his way through them.

Some he watched for ten minutes and when he knew that he could watch no more, they would be ejected, and it would be on to the next one. It was a complete mish mash of viewing. Westerns to thrillers. One or two of them he really enjoyed, especially the Only Fools and Horses collection that made him laugh out loud.

The weeks passed by. School sent out work for him to do and links so that his class could learn virtually together. Billy did not mind; it was nice

that he would see his friends on the many Zoom calls he had to join in school time. And all of the time the DVDs in the box got less and less, until the only ones that were left were the ones that gave no indication about what they were about. Obviously, these were the ones that his Granddad had made by himself, and Lord only knew what was on them!

But when he couldn't face watching another repeat of Top Gear with his dad one night, he grabbed the first DVD he could put his hands on and settled back onto his bed to see what his granddad had deemed worth recording and keeping hold of it.

As he waited for the DVD to load, he scrolled through the messages on the many groups he belonged to on his mobile phone. School friends, football friends, there was even a group with all the youngsters of their little village. Every group had pages and pages of messages on, they were all in the same boat. All their lives were in some sort of limbo and the only way they could keep in touch was via Facebook or Watsapp, Instagram and Snapchat. Suddenly everyone's mobile phones were the most important thing they owned.

Catching up on anything he may have missed out on in the 30 minutes or so that he had last checked, he was shocked when a familiar voice filled his room. 'Without further ado, here is Miss Thompson and her reception class singing 'Away in a Manger.' There was a lot of clapping and lots of little boys and girls filed onto the stage. Mrs Brown had been the headmistress of Billy's primary school and Miss Thompson had been his reception teacher. He could remember Mrs Brown, the lady on the stage of his old school; she was younger, but he would have known her anywhere, she was still head mistress of the village primary school and was a well-known face, although he didn't think she lived in the village herself. Miss Thompson, he remembered too, though not from his reception class. By the time that he was in his last year of primary school, Miss Thompson had become Mrs Harvey and she had been his Year 6 teacher.

Billy moved closer to the television. The recording wasn't the best quality and he wanted to see if he could recognise any of his friends or even himself for that matter. He needn't have worried.

Just as the children settled into 3 little neat rows and Miss Thompson got ready to start them off singing their little carol, one little boy pushed his way through and made his way to the front of the stage.

Billy recognised himself straightaway!!

He couldn't remember singing by himself.

But that was just what he did. Billy could see the 4-year-old version of himself on the screen. He opened his mouth and off he went.......

>Pressure pushing down on me

>Pressing down on me no man ask for

>Under pressure that burns a building down

>Splits a family in two

>Put's people on streets

As the little boy sang on and on, Billy could hear his granddad saying to who would probably have been his grandma 'I didn't know he was doing a solo!!!' It was his grandma, he heard her reply 'I don't think he is supposed to be doing it, look at the teachers faces!!' with that, the camera swung around, and Miss Thompson and Mrs Brown were staring with their mouths wide open at Billy.

His granddad even managed to capture Mrs Brown's hand gesture to leave the little boy, when Miss Thompson went to step forward and go to Billy.

Billy watched the screen and remembered none of it!

No one had even spoken about it. But as he watched as his younger self sang on and on, and from what he could make out, sang it word perfectly, the strangest feeling came over him. He didn't remember, but there was something very familiar about the song, obviously he had heard it lots of times, but this was different, it was like he knew the song. Not just knew it but knew knew it!

Little Billy came to the end and there was a great big cheer and lots of clapping. Then when Mrs Brown and Miss Thompson had every one settle back down, Billy went back to his row and all of the children sang Away in a Manger, but that seemed lame in comparison to what the school hall had heard only moments earlier.

The class finished singing, there was much clapping and cheering and then Miss Thompson led her little class off to the side of the stage and the DVD came to an end.

For the next hour or so Billy watched the DVD over and over again. He googled the lyrics and followed the words his younger self sang. He was word perfect.

It was the most bizarre feeling. There was something but Billy couldn't put his finger on it. But there was definitely something. It was too late at night to ask his mam or dad about what had happened at his Reception Carol Service, but he would. Surely, they would know how he had come to know such a grown-up song at such a little age.

It took Billy a little while to get to sleep. When he did, his dreams were full of flashing lights and cheering crowds. When he woke in the morning, he was even more confused than he had been the night before. But he did remember that Freddie Mercury was the lead singer of Queen, and it was Freddie Mercury that had sang Under Pressure.

It was a puzzle. But it was a puzzle he wanted to unravel, and he had all of the time in the world to do just that.

Chapter 2

The next day, with school Zoom calls done and his mam and dad were sitting having a sneaky glass of something in the garden, Billy asked them if they remembered what had happened at school when he was in reception.

They did they said, but neither of them had been there as they had been trying to win a contract for the business with the council and they hadn't been able to reschedule and that was why the Grandmas and Granddads were there.

No, they hadn't seen it.

Billy soon resolved that by dragging his mam and dad into his room and making them sit on his bed while he started the DVD again for what he thought was the 100th time since the night before.

They both sat opened mouthed as they watched their only son sing his little heart out. They said at the time no one had made a big deal out of it; they had won the contract and what had happened with Billy had basically faded into the background. Watching it though, they thought that maybe they should have seen the DVD earlier.

Back in the garden Billy asked them questions. How did he know the song so well?? Neither his parents knew, they weren't big Queen fans. No, they had never heard him sing it at any time, they didn't even think they had a Queen CD in their vast music collection. Had anything like that ever happened before or after?? The glance at each other was only fleeting, but Billy saw it and as both his mam and dad boo booed off the question and tried to change the conversation to what they should have for lunch. Billy wouldn't let it go.

He may not have got anywhere with them then, but he would bide his time. That old thing called time was what he had plenty of.

Something was stirring within him, but for the life of him he had no idea what. It was a feeling like he already knew the answer but had misplaced it and would need to rummage about within himself until he found it. It was a funny feeling; it was like when sometimes in class his mind would wander off in a geography lesson and when he refocused on the lesson it was like he had actually left the room and had no idea how he got back. But didn't everyone do that?? Was that not day dreaming??

Billy ate his lunch, then with no lessons planned for the afternoon, took a rug, and lay on the grass in the garden and watched the sky as the clouds moved past. It was hot, for being in the middle of a pandemic and everyone having to just stay at home, the weather was unusually kind. If it was a normal time and he had time to kill, it would be raining, and he would be stuck indoors. But for the time being, he was content to just lie and do nothing. There was something on his mind, but for the life of him he could not remember what it was.

He could hear the hustle and bustle of him mam and dad working in the conservatory, they had all the windows and doors open, it would be like a greenhouse in there, but the wheels of industry were still turning slowly, and his mam and dad had to figure out how to keep their business afloat and keep their staff employed.

With the heat, his big lunch and the hum drum of his mam and dad working in the conservatory, Billy could feel his eyes begin to grow heavy. And before he knew it, he was falling asleep lying on a rug in the back garden.

Billy could still feel the warm sun on his face, and he could hear his mam and dad in the conservatory, he was asleep but not asleep, he was more in that limbo land when you weren't quite either.

He had no idea how long he lay there, but something made his heart flip, and his eyes shoot open. Someone had spoken to him. But easing up and looking around the garden, everything as was when he first lay down. His mam and dad were still in the conservatory working and the rest of the garden was deserted. But someone had definitely spoken to him. It must have been a dream Billy thought to himself and settled himself back down, closed his eyes and prepared himself to go back to the land of nod.

And then he heard the voice again. This time it was as clear as day. 'Oh, the sun is beautiful on my face, it feels like I am back in Zanzibar, I can almost smell the spices!'

Billy knew instantly that there was no one in the garden with him. The voice he could hear was coming to him from within his own head. It had a crisp tone to it, posh. Not like how Billy spoke, which wasn't a broad accent but was definitely North Eastern. Geordie. But the voice did sound familiar, he had heard the voice before.

But then it was gone, and all Billy could do was lie on the grass and try and remember where he had been the last time, he had heard the man's voice.

He had no idea, but there was definitely something stirring within him, something that he knew had been normal to him once upon a time but didn't happen anymore. His mam and dad knew something, he had seen the glance between them when he had asked them about singing that song.

But what??? He still had time. He still had time to remember what it was he could not remember lying there in his back garden. The song and the voice. And there was the feeling that there was something else. This time Billy slept… soundly!

Chapter 3

It was almost a week before Billy got opportunity to have a word with his mam. And considering that they all barely left the house, apart to go in walks and deliver food to the Grandmas and Granddads; was amazing.

But Billy had made up his mind that he wanted to have a word with his mam on her own, she was the easiest nut to crack in the way that she was more than likely to tell him if there had been occurrences after his song in Miss Thompson's class. Billy knew for certain that his dad would just brush it away.

So, it wasn't until Billy woke early the following Saturday morning, knowing for sure that his mam would already be up and pottering around did Billy ask his mam 'was that the only thing I did that was strange mam? Singing in Miss Thompson's class?' whilst his mam was loading up the dishwasher and he was munching his way through a bowl of rice crispies.

At first, he thought that his mam was just going to do a dad and brush the question away. She certainly acted as if she hadn't heard him, set the dishwasher away, switched on the kettle and made herself a cup of coffee. But then she sat herself down on a seat next to him and said 'No, Billy, there were a few odd things, up until quite recently! I thought that was the end of them, but that DVD your granddad gave to you seems to have re-ignited whatever it is that or who you thought you were.'

Billy was shocked. He was sure his mam would have said that had been a lone incident. That even though the voice in his head the week before had been so clear and so familiar, his rendition of Under Pressure had been a one off and something that he had probably heard at his Grandmas and Granddads.

His mam went on to say that at first, they thought he had an imaginary friend. His sister had one when she was little, and they assumed this person that Billy talked to and about was something similar. But Billy had been different. Emily's friend had gone before she started school, she had never spoken of it since. Billy's had followed him out of reception, through the infants and junior school and it was only when he went off to secondary school did, he seem to have vanished.

Billy had no memory of any of this. He couldn't remember having a friend that wasn't real!! How couldn't he remember.

'I can't remember mam. I can't remember singing in Miss Thompson's class and last week I heard a voice in my head, and I thought I knew who it was, but I've been thinking about it, and I don't! If my imaginary friend was such a big thing in my life, why don't I remember him, or her!'

Billy's mam had no idea. They had seen a counsellor when he was about 7 years old, she said. But they just said that some children had overactive imaginations and it would go when Billy was more confident. She thought that had happened. When he started playing football and learning piano and got himself a large circle of friends, Billy hadn't talked about any of the things he used to! She wanted to know what the voice in Billy's head had said to him.

When he told her she laughed. 'That makes sense, seems he still with you after all!'

'He?????' Billy asked!

'Yes, he, you said it had a man's voice as well, didn't you?'

'Do you know who he is? Did he have a name?? Did I call him anything mam?' Billy asked, sure that once he had a name, he would remember whatever it was he used to talk about!

'Yes, Billy he had a name, you said that you used to be called Freddie Mercury!'

Seeing the puzzled look on her son's face his mam added 'Freddie Mercury, who was in Queen, who sang that song you sang so perfectly in Miss Thompson's reception class!'

With that the phone rang and within seconds Billy's mam was chatting away to one of the Grandmas'.

At a loss what to do, Billy made his way upstairs, jumped into the shower and tried to think about what his mam had told him. Freddie Mercury!!! He just couldn't remember any of it.

Sitting in his room he Googled Freddie Mercury. There was no way that he could know anything about him when he was 4 years old. If he was just an imaginary friend, then someone would have to have told him about him and he knew for certain that a 4-year-old would have to have an IQ that was out of this world to retain any of the information.

Opening Freddie Mercury's Wikipedia page, he began to read about his Alta ego.

Freddie Mercury Born Farrokh Bulsara on 5th September 1946 died 24th November 1991 – he lived and died even before Billy was born. *Born in Stone Town – Sultanate of Zanzibar*

Zanzibar?? Zanzibar?? Where had he heard that recently. Billy racked his brains trying to remember, he had definitely heard of Zanzibar, but where and when? And then the penny dropped.

A week or so earlier lying in the back garden.

'Oh, the sun is beautiful on my face, it feels like I am back in Zanzibar, I can almost smell the spices!'

It had been Freddie Mercury's voice he had heard when he was drifting off to sleep. That was why it had sounded so familiar. If what his mam had told his was right and up until he was 11 years old or so, he had claimed that he had a friend called Freddie Mercury then that's exactly who it had been.

But some gut instinct made Billy think that Freddie Mercury hadn't been his friend, he would have remembered that. Billy thought that Freddie Mercury was something else. A memory?? An echo?? He wasn't sure, but it was something he would give a lot of thought to over the coming weeks.

But for the time being he had quite enough of Freddie Mercury and Queen and a song called Under Pressure which seemed to be the only song he knew at the minute; it went around and around in his head.

Picking up his X-Box Controller and putting on his earphones he decided it was time to have some fun with friends that were real, it was FIFA time!!!

And for the next few hours that was exactly what Billy did. He was good at FIFA, had a strong team and he was so consumed with playing the game it wasn't until his team got to the tournament final and he subsequently lost did he even give Freddie Mercury a second thought.

But he was back. It gave Billy a fright when the voice in his voice said. 'Well, I never, that's my song. What year is this?? 2020 you say???' Billy had not been aware that he had answered the voice, but he must have because he had told him that the game was called FIFA and it was a computerised football game that he played with his friends. 'Really, all your friends are playing together, and you are not even in the same room!'

And there it was. Billy's friend Jake had won the match and as they paraded around the graphic induced pitch, We are the Champions was playing through the speaker.

Switching off the console and throwing his headphones down, Billy flung himself onto his bed and stared at the ceiling. It was freaking him out!!

Since playing his granddad's DVD there had been something niggling, he thought that maybe he could remember. That Freddie Mercury had been there before, had they been friends?? Billy wasn't sure, but somewhere deep inside, he could remember having conversations with someone, not out loud ones like he would have with his mam or his dad. In his head conversations and he knew without doubt, whoever or whatever it was in his head, would answer back. They talked!!

As Billy lay on his bed, it all began to have a very familiar feel to it. It felt like it had been something that he had locked away, like when you have a nightmare and even though you remember it because it was so scary, you lock it away and try never to think about it ever again.

'It's now or never!' Billy thought to himself as he lay on the bed. 'Freddie?? Are you there??' Billy said in his head. Nothing!!!

He lay a bit longer. Tried again! 'Freddie?? Are you there??' Nothing!!!

Even more confused, Billy jumped off the bed and made his way downstairs to find something to eat. The good thing about living in Lockdown was that there was always a full fridge, loads of snacks and they never seemed to run out of cans of pop. With the regular delivery of supermarket food to the house, there was no waiting around for his mam to run into a shop on her way home from work.

Collecting a small feast, Billy made his way back up to his bedroom to plough his way through it. His mam would have a fit if she saw how much he was eating, she seemed to have turned into some sort of Michelin star chef since they were all her guinea pigs for whatever recipe she had found in one of her many cookery books which up until very recently had basically been for decoration.

Billy had to admit, she was getting better. Just the night before she had made some sort of curry along with homemade nan breads, it had been amazing and whereas leftovers went off to the grandmas and grandads, last night there had been none!!

'Oh, I used to love a good vindaloo, and a chop suey!!'

The voice was there!!

'Is that you Freddie???' Billy asked again!

Of course, it is me, who else would it be??' The voice replied!

And Freddie Mercury was back in Billy Watson's head.

Chapter 4

Having someone in your head talking to you was the most bizarre feeling. But for some reason Billy, it also made him feel safe. He wasn't scared. Confused yes!! How was Freddie Mercury in his head? He was no one special, Billy Watson from Newcastle! But there it was, there he was. The sound of Freddie in his head gave him a feeling of a warm blanket. If he had been there up until a few years ago, what did they talk about?

Billy was older and wiser, and he had lots of questions he needed to ask. But they could wait, tea was ready and even though he had eaten his way through a mountain of rubbish food, he was starving. And whatever it was his mam had concocted for tea that night smelt delicious, there was plenty of time for Freddie Mercury, time was something he had plenty of these days!

Funnily enough, it wasn't until the following day that Billy got chance to have some Freddie time. After tea, the family had played Monopoly and it had been a very sleepy Billy that trundled back up the stairs and into his bed.

Unsure what it was he wanted to know, Billy put on his earphones and found a Queen Essentials Playlist on his mobile phone. Stretched out on his bed he let the music wash over him. He knew the songs, who didn't? Wasn't Bohemian Rhapsody still the most popular song on the planet?? But if he thought that Freddie Mercury was going to give him some sort of running commentary, he was wrong. But as he lay there listening to song after song, he was sure that he could hear humming!!

An hour and a half later, Bohemian Rhapsody was building up for the second time, so Billy stopped the playlist.

'Wasn't that just wonderful!' The voice was back!

Jumping on the opportunity, Billy asked Freddie Mercury how he was in his head!

He had no idea he said. One day there had been nothing but silence and darkness and then the next there had been much frivolity as he seemed to now be some young child. Billy. Freddie said he wasn't sure if he was still supposed to be himself or if something had gone wrong! Was he in fact supposed to be Billy Watson now with no recollection of himself at all? All he knew was that for a few years he lived some sort of childish existence, had funny conversations with Billy and heard glimpses and glances of a new world.

And then one day there had been nothing. A door had closed and even though he could still hear and see things, no one spoke to him. Freddie said he hadn't minded, he watched what was happening in the world with awe, sometimes heard one of his songs which always brought him joy, but until Billy had stirred a memory of him only a few days earlier, the little boy who had been such a joy to know had ceased to believe in his existence, he had just been a passenger!

Freddie had no idea if he would stay with Billy forever, he had no one to ask. There had only ever been him there. He didn't like to think of it as limbo, even with Billy's silence it had been so much better than the darkness and silence that had preceded it, and he certainly had no memory himself as to whether he had been in Heaven or been in Hell. He only knew Billy Watson and the life he lived.

Between the two of them they still knew nothing.

Billy tried to act as normal as possible around the family. He certainly didn't want them to think that because of Lockdown he was regressing into his childhood self. So, he did all the things that he would normally

do, but at the same time read every single article he could find online about Freddie Mercury!

Some fact and some obviously fiction, if the protests inside his head from Freddie were anything to go by. But Freddie was also very humble. After almost 30 years since his death, he was still having an influence on today's society.

Not just with his music. His flamboyant clothes, his sexuality, his teeth. They were all still very much evident. What a legacy!

Billy watched videos on U Tube of the current Queen line up with Adam Lambert. Freddie was impressed, said he really could not have thought of anyone better to step into his very big shoes, seems Freddie was never shy when it came to his musical performances, but he was upset to see his band members as what could only be described as pensioners! But as Billy pointed out to Freddie, they might have been older, but they were still performing, where was Freddie Mercury?? Stuck in a teenager's head. That made Freddie laugh!

They watched Live Aid together, his greatest performance according to Freddie. And they read items about his death and the tributes that were made to Freddie after it. Freddie was quiet for a very long time after that.

Not wanting to intrude, Billy got on with his life.

The days were still warm and even though he had Zoom lessons all day nearly every day, he didn't mind. If his mam thought anything about the conversation they'd had, she didn't mention it, but he sometimes caught her looking at him strangely as if to say, 'what's going on inside that head of yours Billy Watson?' But even if she had asked, he would have said he didn't know. Because he didn't. He undoubtedly had Freddie

Mercury there, but he had no idea why, or how or even if it was a forever thing! Was he the only person that this had ever happened to?? He certainly didn't want to shout it out, he didn't want to put a status on Facebook asking if anyone else had some famous dead person in their head, he would be in counselling before he knew it. But he could be subtle. He could do some internet searches, discreetly so that he didn't have every nut case on the planet contacting him.

With Freddie still quiet, Billy knew that he wasn't huffing or anything, he just needed time to digest all of the information that he and Billy had found out together. Billy began his quest.

Chapter 5

Billy typed into the search engine. Then deleted and retyped, how did you even begin to ask such a bizarre question. In the end he typed 'is it possible to have a dead celebrity's voice in your head?' He hit the return key and waited to see what happened.

Loads of website links came up about reincarnation. It wasn't reincarnation; he had Googled that and that was you actually being that person. Billy Watson was not Freddie Mercury! He scrolled down the page. None of them were what he was looking for. He clicked on one that he thought seemed appropriate only to find himself reading about supernatural and ghosts.

About to give up, a forum link caught his eye. 'Who Said That??'

Worth a go, Billy thought to himself.

'Have You Ever Heard a Famous Person's Voice in Your Head and You Know They Are Dead?? If So, We Would Like to Talk to You!

Interesting. It was a member only type of thing and to join you had to fill a form in and then wait to be approved.

Beyond that there was little information – all seemed very private. Perfect Billy thought to himself as he clicked on the form and began filling in the details. He had nothing to lose and everything to gain, if there were others in a similar position then he needed to talk to them.

It took ages to fill in the form. He was a child so would need parental permission so he added his mam's contact details, hopefully he could have a word with her before they got in touch. Then he had to describe what experience he had and if the person was still with him. Happy that he didn't sound like a fruit loop, he clicked the send button and closed his laptop.

'I do hope that there are others out there too. That we can fathom out why this has happened!' stated Freddie in clipped tones. 'And yes, I have finished licking my wounds, Billy. It was just that everyone said such lovely things!'

Billy was pleased Freddie was back. It would give him a bit courage talking to him mam, he wasn't doing this on his own. And when he suggested that they went for a walk together, his mam couldn't get her trainers on quick enough, it was like she already knew. They walked and they talked, and he told her that Freddie Mercury was back and everything that had happened since they had their early Saturday morning conversation. Especially about the forum he was trying to join the one that he needed her permission to be on. She promised faithfully that she would respond as soon as she had the email, on one condition. That they had no secrets. She wanted to be with him every step of the way, that she knew who he was talking to and what about. Billy could do that. Somehow even having the slightest chance that he wasn't the only one that this dead person in his head thing was making him feel a whole heap better. Even when his mam said she would have to tell his dad nd his sister Emily what was happening, it was okay. It seems that he had always been a bit weird, so what difference would it make now!

Chapter 6

And then they waited. Billy's mam had her confirmation email, but for days and days Billy heard nothing.

He had all but given up when a message arrived on his mobile phone telling him he was now a member of the 'Who Said That? Forum.

Billy had Zoom lessons, but as soon as they were done for the day, he followed the link sent to his email address and after setting up a password he was in!

A big read box flashed at him. 'Welcome Billy! Come say Hi!'

Billy did as he was told and pressed the big red button. Straightaway a bubble flashed on the screen.

'Hi Billy, my name is Joe, welcome. Click here for more information on 'Who Said That?'

Billy clicked the button, and a video came into view waiting to be played.

There was a man maybe in his thirties staring at the camera. Joe, Billy presumed. He looked normal enough, pressed play and then turned the volume up on his laptop.

Hi Folks

My name is Joe Weir and I live just outside of London England. I set up this forum in 2017!

Why?? It may be easier if I tell you, my story.

I was just a normal lad. I did things that all normal young lads do including riding in the back of their mates' cars with no seat belt on.

When I was 20, one of my mates had a car crash. It was not a serious one, but I was in the back, just like I always was with no seat belt on, and I banged my head, firstly off the back of the driver's head rest, but then off the window. I was knocked out. The rest of my friends were ok, but I was rushed to hospital where I was unconscious for a couple of hours. I remembered nothing about it. It wasn't until I heard someone shouting at me did, I even become aware that I had been knocked out.

And that is where the fun started.

Someone was shouting 'Come on Sonny, get up, get up and fight me!!' the voice was shouting over and over, each time a little angrier and a little angrier. I can remember lying there trying my hardest to open my eyes, but they were just so heavy. Anyway, the shouting persisted and eventually I summoned up the strength to open my eyes a little bit and see who the person with the terrible bedside manner was.

But the room was full of women. My mum and my gran and the doctor was definitely a woman.

Confused I had closed my eyes and drifted off into a dreamless sleep. I was on the mend. The shouting stopped and a few days later I was allowed home, with the promise to always wear a seat belt no matter how uncool I thought it was, I may not be so lucky the next time.

And I forgot all about the voice that had been screaming at me to wake up.

For a couple of weeks anyway. Fully recovered, I had arranged to go to the cinema with some friends and they were calling to pick me up. I still only had my provisional licence at that time. Anyway, I clambered into the back seat and was just making myself feel comfortable when a voice said. 'don't be a fool, get that belt on boy!' thinking that it was one of my mates taking the micky, I looked at each of them, but they were all chatting away to each other, none of them looked like they had just scolded me for not putting the seat belt straight on. Fastening up, the voice was back 'that's better, I don't want to be hanging about with no fool!' And then it was gone!

Who Said That??'

But there was nothing and there was no one. As strange as it seemed, I soon forgot about it, and it was months later again as I clambered into the back of my mum's car did, I hear the voice again. 'Don't be a fool, get that belt on boy!' for certain I knew that no one in the car had said it.

There was only my mum and my gran. This voice was definitely male and if I wasn't mistaken had a deep American accent.

I said nothing. Just sat in the back of my mum's Toyota Yaris and thought about what I had heard. Who had said that?

Then a voice spoke as clear as a bell.

'It was me, who else would it be?'

'But who are you?' I said to myself or to the voice, but that isn't strictly true, I didn't say it, I thought it. I thought about it inside my head and the voice answered me back!

'Well, I know who I am, I just don't know who you are, and why the hell am here. Is this England?? You English boy?? Don't you know who am??

I had no idea who the voice belonged to or why it was in my head. I sa in the back of the car and asked questions; all in my head. And the voice answered!

You dead? 'Yes, I think I might be'

You American?   'Yes'

Do I know you?   'Yes, the whole world knows me, I'm the greatest

So, you are famous?? 'Yes, the most famous'

Are you an American President?   'No, but I have sure known some'

Are you a famous actor??   'Noooo, but I can sure put on a good show'

Sportsman??   'Yes, I've told you, I'm the greatest'

I sat and watched the back of my mum and gran's heads as they chatted away, both oblivious to the chatter that I was having with myself!! 'The greatest??' Where had he heard that before???

Do you play baseball??   'No that's for girls'

Football?   'Noooo'

Race Car Driver?   'Do I sound like a race car driver???'

I was at a loss. What the hell was going on. I had taken a bump to my head and had woken up with an obnoxious American in my head. Did I have concussion?? Should I ask my mum to take me back to hospital for a scan on my head??? I was actually having a conversation with myself!!! There was something very wrong!!

'I'm as confused as you are boy. I think I was dying; I think I died, it was very dark for a long time, I think I had my eyes shut. Then I opened them, and I was here with you. I have no idea how I got here or where I am. I can see what you see and can distantly hear what is being said about me, but mainly I can hear you. If you speak to me directly, I hear o as clear as the bell. So don't be thinking that this is all about you. I'm a dead black man living in some snotty English boy's head!!'

Okay, okay, we just go to figure out what this is all about. There must be some sort of explanation!! You say you are a famous sportsman, American sportsman, you are going to have to help me out here, I barely know any English sportsmen so the chances of me knowing who you are very low!!

It took a little while for the voice to answer.

'What if I said "Float like a butterfly, sting like a bee"'

I had it in an instant, even with all my American sportsmen ignorance, I knew who had used that quote!!

'Muhammad Ali?????? You are Muhammad Ali????'

'Seems I used to be, now I'm just a noise!'

And that was that. I had no idea how the voice got there. Was this a permanent condition? Was he just a figment of my imagination? But to me he seemed as real as a person at the end of a telephone. I couldn't see him, but I could talk to him, and he could talk back to me. I officially became a weirdo!

He stayed. He is still with me. I never spoke to anyone about him. But I did question him endlessly about his life. I made notes and then when he complained that he was sick of talking I would check out what he had told me. He was always 100% accurate.

He could be loud and arrogant. He would often fly off the handle with me, not always when it was about him, but something I did, or I said. But mainly we talked. To be honest he wasn't that long dead, but I would speak about how people still talked about him, I became a bit of an expert on boxing and the rest of sport in general. And he told me about being a black man in America. And over the months and years we became friends.

But my curiosity was piqued. Was I the only one that this had happened to? I was not Muhammed Ali, but he was certainly with me. The bump on the head had happened very shortly after Muhammed had died, was that why??

I began to do some research. It was a very grey area. There were lots of people claiming to be a famous dead person. But when I scratched the surface of these people, they weren't, they just wanted to stand out in the crowd.

So, I decided to go all out and create this forum, in the hope that if there were others like me, they would somehow find their way to it. I only wanted the genuine weirdos!

The forum was set up. And I waited and I waited. I began to think that it had been a mistake and there was only me that this had happened to. I had tried and failed. I had paid for a year's subscription so decided to leave it up but my obsession with it waned and I got on with my life and my relationship with Muhammed Ali!

And then one day I got an email notification. It was from someone called Ann Wheeler and she was interested in the forum. At last, someone had actually reacted. Email fired back off to her, I waited again.

Ann emailed her telephone number and keeping my mind as open as possible, I called her.

We talked for a very long time. At first, I was nervous about what to say, I did not want to sound like a lunatic. She sounded a lot older than me, so I let her lead the conversation. Yes, of course I had heard of Amelia Earhart …… and we were off!

I won't bore you with the details. You can see for yourself on the forum the hows and wheres and whos!!

All I know is that from the moment I spoke to Ann Wheeler, I did not feel so bad. And after Ann contacted me and we became two people in the forum, others began to come too. And now we have over 400 active members, all with their own unique story to tell.

To be honest, even with all of the discussions we have had together, individually or as a group, I am no more enlightened about it all than I was in the beginning when Muhammed Ali first opened his mouth as I lay in that hospital bed.

I still get scared when I think about it, or worse still when I forget about it and get a fright all over again when a voice in my head shouts at me. But now I know that all I have to do is come to the forum and there is always someone there to talk about it all too. Makes me feel less strange.

You have come to the right place. We are quite a community. And believe it or not we even manage to have some laughs together. Especially when one of the voices takes offence at another. When we all together it seems to make the voices greater, if that makes sense.

Anyway, make yourself at home. All I ask you to do is do what I have done and make yourself a little video introducing yourself and of course who your friend is. Maybe how all this started for you, the more we all know about this, then maybe one day we might be able to figure it out.

You can upload your video through the portal. Fill in the information boxes and then you are good to go. Watch the videos, join the meetings, read the blurbs, talk to individuals, everyone is checked and vetted and basically in the same boat as yourself.

Any problems, I'm here. You are in the right place; please enjoy!

The video ended and Billy scrolled. down the page and read the rest of the blurb!

Joe Weir
London

'Who Said That? Muhammad Ali Said That!'

Muhammad Ali – Born Cassius Clay
17th January 1942 – 3rd June 2016
Kentucky USA
Professional Boxer

Legacy
Time Magazine named Ali one of the 100 Most Important People of the 20th Century.

Muhammad Ali Centre – peace, social responsibility, respect, and personal growth.
Muhammad Ali Boxing Reform Act 2000 – to protect the rights and welfare of boxers in the United States with MMA added in 2016.

61 Professional Fights – 56 wins!!!

Wow!!!!

Chapter 7

There was a button that said meet the members – Billy clicked on it!

There were pages and pages and pages of members. Each had a little photograph of themselves, their name, location and their 'Who Said That??'.

Billy's heart was thumping hard. There were so many of them. He could have spent hours and hours just reading the blurbs.

But he had promised his mam no secrets and now that he was onto the forum, he wanted her to see what it was about. So, taking his laptop downstairs, he found his mam at her makeshift desk in the conservatory and asked her to watch Joe's video.

The video ended and Billy's mam grabbed hold of her son and cuddled him in tight. She was trying to kiss the top of his head, but these days he was a good couple of inches taller than her so ended up kissing his forehead. It didn't matter, it had been a long time since they'd had a cuddle. And she was crying. But through the tears she was laughing. 'Wait until your dad sees this, you know how he loves his boxing!! Muhammad Ali, that is amazing. We need to do a video don't we?? I'll film it for you and help you will the bits in if you like??'

Billy did like and that's what they did. Together they managed to make a decent copy of the DVD of Miss Thompson's Reception Nativity play on his mobile phone, that would make a good starting point his mam said.

Then after that, Billy's mam held his mobile phone as Billy introduced himself to the world, along with his 'Who Said That?'.

They both watched Billy's video a couple of times and agreed it would do. Billy looked and sounded nervous, but he would no matter how many times they recorded it, he certainly didn't have a flamboyant

Freddie Mercury side who could switch it on for an audience at the drop of a hat, and who throughout the thing had remained tight lipped inside Billy's head. He had been on his own for this one for once.

And the last bit had been the blub!

Billy Watson
Newcastle

'Who Said That? Freddie Mercury Said That!'

Freddie Mercury- Born Farraokh Bulsara
6th September 1946 – 24th November 1991
Stone Town, Sultanate of Zanzibar
Singer Songwriter

Legacy
Lead Localist of rock band Queen
Regarded as one of the greatest lead singers of rock music
300 million record sales

Bohemian Rhapsody & We Are The Champions voted greatest song of all time
Death helped highlight Aids

Satisfied that they had done everything they could for the forum, the laptop was closed and the rest of the day, there was no talk of Freddie Mercury, Muhammad Ali or the 'Who Said That?' Forum.

Chapter 8

For Billy Watson life virtually continued as normal, or a normal as was possible during a worldwide pandemic, with Thursday night clapping on the doorstep for all of the heroes of the NHS and people working throughout the lockdown. There was talk of restrictions being lifted somewhat, or families being able to bubble together and the 2m distance rule. But for the time being, it was business as usual.

His mam and dad had began working again. There had been funding and they had bought protective clothing and such like for the staff and they were still using the conservatory as their office, but the staff were back working again and there was hope that the business could survive whatever was thrown at it in the coming months.

Billy joined his first Zoom Forum on 'Who Said That?'

Unsure at first, he had hummed and haa'ed all day. It had been Freddie who had talked him into doing it. 'You might learn something, you always thought it was just you and I, but there are others, should we not try this meeting and see what others have to say about it all??' So, at 7pm he had clicked on the link and became a little square on a screenful of faces, just like he was with his classmates.

Everyone welcomed new member Billy, but they didn't force him to speak, he just waved at everyone and that seemed to be enough.

For the remainder of the meeting, he listened with interest as first Joe, who was founder and seemed leader of the Forum, told stories of their lives and what they had been getting up to with their 'friends'.

There were people from all over the place, not just the United Kingdom, there was a lady from Spain and a couple from the United States who

had both either stayed up late or got up really early to join the discussion or as they liked to call it the chat. And the people were all sizes and shapes too, ages, backgrounds. It seemed that these friendships they all had with the famous people in their heads were not stuck to any demographic.

Billy found himself laughing out loud a few times. It was so weird listening to people talk often in what was it called, the third person. 'He said she said'. And Joe had been right in his introductory video when he said it made the voices greater, all the while Billy was on the call, Freddie Mercury was chattering away in his head. 'Who did he say that he had?', 'That's impossible, that person isn't even dead'. Freddie was doing his own little running commentary.

There was a girl talking, she didn't seem to be much older than Billy, but she spoke confidently and was telling the room about a trip she had taken into an Apple shop earlier in the year. How that the voice in her head had made her ask ridiculous questions to the young boy that was serving her and how she had left the shop red faced and empty handed. She'd had no idea what she had been asking about, but it was something very technical and very outdated. She was laughing on the screen, she said that he was making it impossible for her to buy anything technical because he shouted at her so loudly, she always ended up sounding like a gibbering wreck!

Billy was fascinated. Freddie was shouting in Billy's head, 'who was it?? Who was it?' But the girl was finishing off her story and Billy only got chance to glimpse her name, Jess Jenkins. But she was on the forum so Billy would be able to find her and put Freddie Mercury at ease.

The next hour was much the same. They all seemed to have stories where their voice poked their noses into their everyday lives. Billy supposed he was lucky, Freddie was just there, sometimes he would hum along to one of his own songs if he heard it, but to date he had never overpowered Billy, apart from Miss Thompson's Reception Nativity that is.

Meeting over, they all waved to reach other, then one by one the little boxes disappeared, and Billy was left staring at a blank screen.

He felt ok though. They had all been in the same boat and it was a nice feeling knowing that he wasn't the only person that it was happening to. He wasn't sure that he would ever talk out loud in the group, but he had been happy listening to other people. It was nice to belong he supposed.

Thinking that was it for the night, Billy was about to close his laptop when there was a little ping which seemed to mean someone wanted to chat with him.

Andrew Storey   Hi!

Billy clicked on the little message button and replied   Hi

Andrew Storey   How did you find tonight? It was your first forum, wasn't it??

Billy Watson   Yes – it was good. I wasn't sure what it was all going to be about.

Andrew Storey   I don't think you live far from me – I'm in Sunderland

Billy Watson   No not far at all – but a million miles at the minute.

Andrew Storey   Yes strange times. I've been on this forum about a year. Obviously much more now that we are stuck in the house. But I like it and everyone really nice!

Billy Watson   Yes it seems to be good. It has made me feel a bit better.

Andrew Storey   Listen, I have to go now, having a takeaway delivered and there is a film on telly I want to watch. But let's chat soon. Have a look at my video and blurb when *you get a minute. And drop me a message when you want to talk. Nice to know you aren't the only one, isn't it? Speak soon.*

Then he was gone, and Billy was once again looking at a blank screen.

With no takeaway being delivered or film on the telly he wanted to watch, he clicked on Andrew Story and read his blurb.

Andrew Storey
Sunderland

'Who Said That? Walt Disney Said That!'

Walter Elias Disney

5th December 1901 – 15th December 1966

Chicago Illinois USA

Animator, Film Maker, Entrepreneur

Legacy

Cultural Icon
59 Academy Award Nominations
22 Academy Awards

3 Golden Globe Nominations
2 Special Achievement Awards
1 Emmy Award
Hollywood Walk of Fame

'Oh wow!!!' Billy said to himself. 'Wow indeed!!' Freddie Mercury answered.

He clicked on Andrew Storey's video!

Hi everyone, my name is Andrew Storey, and I am from Sunderland.

As you can see from my blub, my 'Who Said that?' is Walt Disney!!

Cool I hear you say, one of the greatest or as he says, the greatest animator that has ever lived. But trust me, this man inside my head is a pure perfectionist and boy does he let me know it.

There was no bump to the head for me. Walt Disney has always been there. I didn't know who he was in the beginning, far too young to understand, there was just a man in my head who talked a lot, especially when I was watching cartoons.

My mam said that when I was old enough to talk, I used to shout, 'be quiet I can't hear the telly!' There was no one ever there except me and my mam. She said that she had raised concerned with my health visitor, who assured her it was quite normal for a small child to have an

imaginary friend, especially an only child with no one else to play with. So, I was left to get on with it and by the time I had started school, the voice in my head was someone that I and I alone acknowledged.

I discovered who it was quite by chance.

My mam had taken me to the pictures to see Aladdin, I must have been about 7 or 8 at the time. The voice was extremely vocal, so much so that I really didn't have a clue what was going on in the film. The chatter was all about the animations, the colour, the sound quality, the music. The film obviously wasn't up to the voice's standards. And he was making sure I heard about it.

The credits came up and the voice was very annoyed indeed, saying how his name should never have been used unless the film was up to his high standards.

'His name????' I thought to myself. As the credits rolled there were so many names, but only one name that really mattered. Walt Disney!!!

'Eureka!!!' The voice called in my head.

And that folks as they say was that.

No idea why he is here!! No idea how he got here! But for all my life I have had an opiniated old man in my head who over the years has become something of a friend.

I have lost count of the amount of Disney films I have watched, I am quite the expert, and the older ones are the easier ones to sit through, although he is very critical of himself, but the newer ones that have been produced under the 'Walt Disney' name, boy can they be an experience!!

Having Walt Disney isn't something I tell many people about. My mam knows, she almost put me into counselling, and she also did what any responsible parent who had a child that claimed to have Walt Disney in his head would do; she spoke to a fortune teller. Whatever it was she heard from the fortune teller worked, because my mam became as accepting to the situation as I was.

All I could do was embrace him. I became an engineer, remember Walt Disney created some of the best theme parks in the world, he likes to know how things work, which was a God send to me when I was doing my degree, he was my secret weapon with his methodical approach towards problem solving.

And of course, I know every single Disney Princess by name, which believe it or not can make you a bit of a hit with the ladies! Just ask my wife!

I have small children of my own now. So far there doesn't seem to be any one special in their heads, but I continue to watch, as does my wife. Beside my mam and you lot, she is the only other person that knows about Walt!!

So, my advice. Make the most of your voice, they chance to know an awful lot about an awful lot. They aren't famous for nothing!!

And enjoy the show!

'This is all really interesting' Billy said to himself, but then wasn't surprised when a voice chirped up 'We still don't know why I am here though do we? And it seems that although you have found lots of people the same as us, they don't know either! Will I never rest in peace?' Billy could hear the tinkle of laughter in Freddie's voice and knew that although he was curious about why he was there, he didn't mind. Hadn't he said that it had been dark before Billy?? So surely this existence was better than nothing!

Anyway, that Andrew says that I should learn from you!! What skills can I learn from you then Freddie???' But Freddie Mercury didn't respond, he sometimes got like that, went quiet, or maybe he just didn't have anything to teach Billy!

Chapter 9

Far too wired to think about sleep, he scrolled through the pages and pages of faces, he was looking for that girl, the one from the Apple store. Jess Jenkins!!! There was no rhyme or reason to the order of the faces, they weren't in alphabetical order by person or voice, maybe they were by the date they joined the forum, it was all just a jumble!

There were so many people he wanted to stop and look at. So many faces and so many famous names, but to be fair, a lot of them he had never heard of, but they were famous for a reason so he would check them out, at some point. But first he wanted to know about Jess and who it was that made her talk gibberish in the Apple store.

There were just so many faces!! About to give up and have a read of someone else; he saw her name!

Jess Jenkins
Maidstone

'Who Said That? Alexander Graham Bell Said That!'

Alexander Bell
3rd March 1847 – 2nd August 1922
Edinburgh Scotland
Inventor, Scientist and Engineer

<u>Legacy</u>
Patented the first telephone
Inventor of Metal Detector
Billy pressed on the video and Jess Jenkins sprang into life.

Hello Everyone. My name is Jess Jenkins and I'm from Maidstone in Kent.

I too have a voice in my head. He is a Scottish gentleman who in my opinion invented the greatest thing ever – the telephone!

He is Alexander Graham Bell!!

How amazing is that??? Something that every single person on the planet uses everyday was the idea of the man that lives inside my head.

I don't know when he got there! I don't think he was there when I was little, I don't remember him. But by the time I got to secondary school he made himself very known to me!

I didn't have a bump on the head or anything, but when I stepped up to secondary school, I was bullied quite a bit. I think maybe the trauma of that period triggered something. Anyway, one day I returned from school and made for my bedroom just as I always did. I was very upset, there was a gang of girls who seemed to take pleasure in making my life a misery, made worse by my primary school best friend being part of the gang. Anyway, I was crying when a voice said, 'Don't be worrying about all this lassie, they will lose interest, don't let them change you!' 'Who Said That?' I thought to myself. I was alone in my room, alone in the house.

'I do not want to scare you more than you already are, but my name is Alexander and for some questionable reason, I appear to be alive in your mind.'

Talk about being freaked out!!! If I was being bullied for being a freak up until then, what would I be if I had voices in my head??

But the voice spoke again.

'if you do not mind me asking, are you deaf by any chance??

'Just in one ear!!' I said to myself. But the voice had heard it. 'Oh, I see. Both my mother and my wife were profoundly deaf, that was the reason I became interested in hearing and speech in the first place!'

I had been born deaf in one ear, some of the pipes hadn't fused together. Allegedly it would be a mammoth operation with no guarantee that it would even be successful, so my mum and dad had decided against it, and I had grown up with only my right ear working.

It hadn't really affected me, although sometimes if someone was on the wrong side of me, I didn't hear them. But as I had grown up, I had *managed perfectly fine, and it was just part of who I was. Sometimes people thought I was ignorant, but those who knew me knew just to gently turn my head and all would be well.*

That was why I took the girls bullying me at secondary school so badly, Kate had always known about my condition, it had never been an issue. But the new girls took the micky, they would cock their heads to one side like a dog and pull a dumb looking face at me. When Kate had started doing it too it was too much.

'People can be so cruel. But while I am here, I will do what I can to help you!'

And that is just what he did. He heard everything. From then on in there was no need for me to turn my head or have my head turned. Alexander heard everything on the left and if he thought I had missed it, he would say it to me! He is my hero and my friend.

Not that it is was always a good thing as I got older.

The bully relented. With Alexander in my head, I felt braver, fearless. They continued to taunt me, but whereas before I would become upset, Alexander's reassurance in my head made me ride above them. And as with all bullies, when they couldn't cause me anymore misery, they lost interest and they moved on to someone or something else.

I never spoke to Kate again.

But like I said it wasn't always a good thing having Alexander with me all of the time. Boyfriends were a problem.

You see Alexander was born in a different lifetime. Women and girls didn't have the freedom they have nowadays. So, a boyfriend whispering sweet nothings in my ears would send Alexander tail spinning. Or late-night chats with friends about what we had all been getting up to. Alexander would be tut tutting in my head, but I learned to ignore him. And I learned how to distract him.

You see the Alexander in my head was Alexander Graham Bell who invented the telephone!

He is a genius! And over the years he plotted the telephone and its humble beginnings up until modern day and all the advancement it has made to today's society.

As much as Alexander has learned off me, I have learned off him. Less about technology, that was never going to be my bag. More about people. About acceptance. About humankind.

I used to think myself odd for having a voice in my head. I am odd, because aside from you lovely people I know of no others. But it also gives me an extra layer. Of protection, Alexander continues to be my deaf ear, but also an understanding of people. So much so that I hope to go to university and obtain a degree in Sociology. I only hope that Alexander Graham Bell continues this journey with me, because as unsure as I am about how he got here, I have no idea when he will leave too!

I look forward to meeting you all, hearing your stories and meeting your 'Who Said That?'

Billy was flabbergasted. Alexander Graham Bell, even he had heard of him. No wonder she ended up talking gibberish in the Apple store. Jess Jenkins wasn't much older than him. He sent her a chat message. 'Watched your video; awesome!'

Unsure if it was because life was so boring in lockdown, or he was genuinely fascinated with these people, but he was loving this forum and couldn't wait to show his mam. He was sure his mam would be reassured that Billy wasn't the only fruit loop on the planet.

It was late, but one more wouldn't hurt, not like he had to be up for anything the following morning, and he was learning. Each video he watched and blurb he read basically taught him something he didn't know. Muhammed Ali, Walt Disney, Alexander Graham Bell. All people he had never really paid much attention to. Now he would. They were of Freddie's world. Stuck inside someone's head, dead but not dead. Living and breathing but as a shadow not an entity!

Billy was doing some deep thinking!!!

Chapter 10

One more before bed. But who!

Then a man caught his eye. He looked like one of the Hairy Bikers off the television.

He clicked on the image!

Neil Charlton
Leeds

'Who Said That? Emily Bronte Said That!'

Emily Bronte
30th July 1818 – 19th December 1848
Thornton, Yorkshire, England
Novelist and Poet

Legacy
Wuthering Heights

Billy had read Wuthering Heights only the year before for English Literature. It had been such a hard read, in the end he had cheated and found a film version, watched it twice and then went back to the book. It had been easier. Neil Charlton certainly didn't look the type to be reading Wuthering Heights; this will be interesting Billy thought as he clicked on Neil's video.

I'm Neil Charlton, from Leeds and don't be put off by my appearance, I have a delicate Yorkshire Rose in my head that goes by the name of Emily Bronte!!

How had she got there?? No idea! I know that she wasn't there until I was about 10, about the time I took my first Holy Communion. As anyone who knows, the lessons and Praise before such a rite of passage are enormous. But I cannot remember her being there as I learnt my scriptures, but she was thereafter.

Again, never judge a book by its cover; I used to be a choir boy!! I had some pipes on me. Anyway, the choir was popular, and we often went to sing at other Churches for weddings, funerals and festivals. One time we went to Haworth which isn't far from Bradford. Anyway, there we were all sitting in the stalls, we had sung a few hymns and just as I knelt down to prayer, I heard someone say, 'you have a beautiful voice!' I sneaked a look about, low and behold if the choir master found you looking around or daydreaming. There were no females around, just my fellow singers, the choir master and the vicar standing to the side of us. All the females there were in the congregation and there would have been no chance of me being able to hear them even I the had shouted. This voice had been more like a whisper!

It unnerved me and all of the rest of the service and on the coach journey home, I kept my ears pin back!

I heard nothing more. Until the next time I sang and at the end there was the voice again 'you sing so beautifully!' 'Who Said That?' But the voice was gone again. But then the next time I sang it was there again. It was the singing that triggered it. I knew for certain that there was no one in the physical world talking to me. It was inside my head. I was going nuts.

But I was curious!

So, I sang, and she talked. That was how it worked.

It wasn't normal, was it? I sat down a few times to talk to my mum and dad about it, but just like the voice in my head, when I opened my mouth to talk about it, I just couldn't find the words.

She loved my singing, so I started to make excuses not to go to choir; sore throat, headache and instead of singing chorister music, I played rock music, as loud and obnoxious as I possibly could and sang along to that. That kept the voice quiet!

It was the beginning of a lifelong love of rock for me and a putrid hatred of it for Emily!

As awkward as it seemed though, after weeks of AC/DC and Black Sabbath curiosity got the better of me once again and I went back to the choir, I missed my friends there. I sang and she was back and for some unknown reason, I was pleased she hadn't gone!

I still hadn't told a soul about the voice. What would I say that wouldn[t] result in a trip to the doctors? I needed to know more about the voice.

So, I started talking directly to her. Who was she? Why was she there

'My name is Emily. I, well, I have no idea why I am with you. All I can recall is that I heard singing and then I was here. Here I assume being some type of being within you. I ascertain that it was your voice I coul[d] hear!'

I was at a loss. Emily!! She spoke like me, with a Yorkshire lilt, I coul[d] hear her dropping the same vowels, but she spoke in almost a whisper so I had to listen really hard to make out the words.

'Where was it you were singing? What was the place called?' Emily asked.

'Mmmm I'm not sure, we visit a lot of places, but I can find out! Are you dead then??' I asked.

'Yes, I think the year of my departing was the winter of 1848. Althoug[h] for sure I'm not sure if it was the following year. I think that I was in my 30th year!'

Almost 200 years ago I thought to myself. How was someone who ha[d] lived over two centuries ago manage to have a conversation with me inside my head?? I could barely hold a conversation with my grandparents who were not only living but were born this century. I couldn't be making it all up.

At the next choir practice, I checked the diary, it had all the dates and bookings in. scrolling back through the pages I found what I was looking for. St Michael and All Angels Church, Haworth.

Choir practice done, I was walking home when the voice said, 'My father was parson at St Michael and All Angels Church, I lived there, I would have been buried there!'

Okay, we were getting somewhere. Somehow the ghost of Emily had got into my head! Probably when I was hitting a high note with my mouth wide open. Even though it was a ridiculous notion, it didn't seem so bad, not so scary as losing his marbles.

'Do you have a second name?' I asked. I wasn't singing but had the feeling that she was still there.

'Second name?' she questioned.

'A surname?' I replied.

'Oh, I see, Bronte. My name is Emily Bronte!'

I had heard that name before. Wasn't there a museum somewhere near, the Bronte Museum? There were some sisters, they were quite famous in these parts, well not just these parts, they had written some films or something!

'Are you famous for something, a film?' I asked her!

'A film?? I am unsure what that is, but my sisters and I wrote poetry and literature, and we were published!' All of this was said in a whisper, but I could hear the pride and pain in her voice!

'What did you write then? I might know it!'

'I wrote a piece called Wuthering Heights and my sister Charlotte wrote Jane Eyre and my sister Anne wrote Agnes Grey and The Tenant of Wildfell Hall. I very much doubt you will know them!'

That was true, he didn't. Not personally, he wasn't a great reader. But he had heard of Wuthering Heights and Jane Eyre, they were films!

'My God, you are so famous!!!!' I screamed at Emily!!

I tried to explain best I could about how they were famous. That not just for books but that there had been films made, movies! Then had to explain what a film was. Emily was shocked and humbled and a little upset.

And the rest like you say is history. Emily Bronte is still in my head. She is very shy and a little timid and every time I have shown her any of her influence over the years, we have been together she retreats into silence.

Kate Bush's rendition of Wuthering Heights sent her silent for weeks. But she did ask to listen again and again when she reconnected.

To this day, I am still unsure if she can see what I can. But we have watched screen adaptions of all of the Bronte sisters works.

Oh, and she loves animals. If it was a thing, I would say that she can talk to the animals!!

I stumbled across this fact quite by chance. I opted to work at the local RCPCA for my work placement. Not because I loved animals, but it was literally at the end of my street, and I had an aunt that worked there. Easy option.

On the first morning I turned up for my shift and was confronted with a huge German Shepherd who seemed to take an instant dislike to me and approached me with teeth bared and a look that made me think that I was about to get my face bitten off.

And then there was Emily. I couldn't hear what she was saying. Her usually whisper was even quieter, there was just a drone. Whatever it was she was moaning on about seemed to be audible to the German Shepherd because all at once the snarl was gone and instead of looking like he wanted to bite me, he began licking my hand. He became a pussy cat!

That theme continued throughout my work placement. All the animals seemed to roll over and want their tummies rubbed the moment they were anywhere near me.

Emily said nothing about it. But I heard the mumblings constantly. She was a horse whisperer.

So impressed with me and my ability to calm down the animals I was offered a job when I left school. All thanks to Emily!!

And now I have boarding kennels of my own. It has turned out to be a very successful venture. Again, all thanks to Emily, whatever it is that she does, the animals respond. An anxious dog becomes more confident, a vicious cat becomes more playful.

I don't know how she got here, but I know that I will be a bit buggered without her.

We sometimes have some time out. I listen to rock music and Emily retreats into some small corner of my mind. The separation has helped us over the years.

I have told no one about Emily Bronte in my head. I have searched for years for an explanation but there hasn't been one. Until I found 'Who Said That?' I thought that I was the only person on the planet that this had happened to. But look at us all.

Whatever or whoever you have, listen to what they have to say, chances are they much cleverer than any of us, Emily is!!

This time Billy turned off his laptop or else he would have been clicking on someone else and would have been there all night.

Neil Carter was right; it was better to know he was one of many and not some sort of solo weirdo. He would show his mam the videos he had watched tomorrow. And his dad and sister too. Emily still hadn't spoken to him about what was going on, maybe it would be a good excuse to open up the conversation.

But for that night, he turned off the lights, hopped into bed and closed his eyes.

'Night Freddie, that was some night, wasn't it?'

'Goodnight Billy, I really don't know what to make of it all. But I am enjoying the videos!! More tomorrow I say!'

With that Billy fell asleep.

Chapter 11

The Lockdown restrictions were beginning to lift slightly. There was word that the school would be reopening with limitations. Billy's mam and dad were talking of going back to their business premises and in a couple of weeks they would be allowed out as long as the 2-metre rule was in place. It was all very exciting.

Billy was true to his word and showed the 'Who Said That?' forum to the family. It became the main topic of conversation around the dinner table for weeks! Everyone had a 'wish list' about who they wanted to watch. But Billy was just doing his own thing, more based on the Zoom calls that he was now a regular participant in.

And Emily and him had the chat. It was awkward at first. She had watched the videos that he had watched so far. When it was over, she simply said 'you're not the freak I thought you were then?' it broke the ice and they talked. Emily could remember vividly Billy talking about Freddie Mercury when he was younger. She said he used to have whole conversations with himself, well one-sided ones. Sometimes he would be sitting giggling when there was nothing to giggle about.

But it was better this time, he wasn't talking out loud. She did say that sometimes she would look at him and he would be miles away, obviously having a conversation in his head. When she said he was lucky, Billy was flabbergasted.

'You are friends with Freddie Mercury, do you know how amazing that is. I know it isn't perfect, you can't really tell anyone, but we all know and in my book that makes you pretty special. And I'm loving watching all the videos of your new friends. Mind if you come across Heath Ledger, I want to have a word with him. How many times have I watched 10 Things I Hate About You and a Knights Tale, and you love Joker!'

Emily bounced out of the room just like she would have done if she had been in to borrow his charger, not talk about the famous person that lived in his head.

Billy had a Zoom call with Jess Jenkins. She was the nearest in age to him whose video and blurb he had met so far.

He was a bit shy at first. But she was nice and soon had him laughing out loud at some of the stuff that she told him about Alexander Graham Bell. He certainly seemed a character. And Jess was blown away with Freddie Mercury, who all the time Billy chatted with Jess was chatted away. Billy could actually feel him shaking his peacock feathers when Jess said he was awesome!

Billy felt much better after talking to Jess. She was only a few years older than him, mainly managed to keep Alexander Graham Bell to herself, but like Billy had gained a lot by joining the 'Who Said That?' forum and mixing with people in the same boat.

Promising that they would keep in touch, the call ended, and Billy decided that he would have a read at some of the other people on the pages and pages of members.

Ann Wheeler!! Billy knew that name. Wasn't Ann Wheeler the woman who was the first to contact Joe Weir when he set up the forum??

Billy clicked on her!

Ann Wheeler
Southampton, England

'Who Said That? Amelia Earhart Said That'

Amelia Earhart
24th July 1897 – 2nd July 1937 (disappeared) – 5th January 1939 (presumed dead)
Atchison, Kansas, USA
Aviation Pioneer, writer

Legacy
First Female Aviator to fly solo across the Atlantic
Promotor of Commercial Travel
Feminist Icon
National Aviation Hall of Fame
National Women's Hall of Fame

Billy knew who Amelia Earhart was. He had seen Night in the Museum and she had been in that, or a character of her was.

Button pressed. Ann Wheeler's video began to play.
Hello, I'm Ann Wheeler and I can tell you the exact date that my 'Who Said That?' got into my head.

It was 28th March 1982, almost 40 years ago.

The reason that I remember it so precisely is because it was the date that I gave birth to my children.

You see I was in hospital, and I have just delivered my beautiful baby boy. He was my first born and it had been a traumatic experience. I had not really known what to expect. My own mother had died years earlier, I only had brothers and none of my friends had children of their own at that point. So, despite reading all of the books, I had been ill prepared for what having a baby was all about.

It hurt so much. The midwife's said baby was lying awkwardly, but they had managed to turn him and after what seemed like hours and hours, he arrived safe and well. Much smaller than the size of my bump would have led to believe, I thought that I would have been giving birth to a baby elephant.

Babe in arms, I was inspecting all of his fingers and toes when an almighty pain shot through my body.

All of a sudden there was pandemonium in the room. Midwifes here there and everywhere. The baby was whipped away from me and truly just in time, another pain ran through me, and I had an almighty urge to push again.

I was panicking, was I dying???

My husband hadn't been with me. The baby had arrived earlier than we had expected, and he was away on business, so in my head I was going to die in that room with no one and no one to look after my son!

A voice was shouting at me. 'You aren't going to die! Come on you can do this. Teeth together an get on with it'

'Who said that?' Though half closed eyes I looked around the room. There was a midwife and a doctor, neither of them looked like they were engaging with me, they were reading through my notes and had a look of shock on their faces.

'Come on, the quicker you do as your told the quicker this will all be over!' the voice said again. No one was saying this to me out loud, it was in my head.

'Come on, push, push, push!!!' The voice shouted at me.

And that's what I did. With all my force I pushed as hard as I could! The voice continued to shout encouragement at me.

'Come on push, push, push, pant, pant, push…….' On and on she shouted and that was what I did and within minutes, the midwife who had been looking so worried moments earlier was smiling at me and handing me another baby.

This time a girl.   My daughter!

'Oh my, she is very beautiful, isn't she??' The voice was still there as I gazed down at another little bundle in my arms.

My head sunk into the pillows. I was exhausted. Baby girl was reunited with her baby brother in the crib, and I slept.

By the time I woke up, both babies were cleaned up and in blue and pink baby grows respectively. I hadn't known what I was having so had one of each in my little hospital bag, never for a second thinking I would need one of each. Both babies were small, but not small enough to need any special care, they were fast asleep in the crib next to me.

I was shell shocked.

The doctor came to see me. The second baby must have been hiding behind the first, they couldn't have known. Even the scan I'd had hadn't shown anything and their heartbeats must have been in sync because they had never heard two heartbeats. It happened sometimes he said, but rarely.

We were moved onto the ward with the rest of the new mammies. In a couple of days, we would be able to go home, providing the three of us were fit and well.

And so overnight, we became a family of four.

I thought the voice in my head had been due to the gas and air that I had taken such a liking to while I'd been delivering my son. But late that night it was there again.

'You were so, so brave. You did so well. Your children are beautiful!'

It was definitely in my head. What the hell. Could it be my mammy from beyond the grave, after all I was her only daughter? Had she come to help me knowing that I was in so much trouble. But my mammy was Irish, and the voice was truly not Irish. It sounded American!!

'Don't be scared. I really have no idea why I am here, but I seemed to have arrived in the nick of time, didn't I?'

'Who are you?' I whispered to myself. It was late and the other new mammies were all asleep. I didn't want them to think I was having some sort of episode. It was obvious that it was only me who could hear the voice so maybe she could hear my thoughts.

'Oh hello, you are still awake, you have had such an exhausting day. My name is Amelia. Perhaps you have heard of me, I was quite the adventurer back in the day. Amelia Earhart!'

'Amelia Earhart who was the first woman to fly?' I asked, unsure if I had heard her right!!

'The very one! Oh, I am so pleased you know about me. I assume that I'm not still in 1937!'

And there she was and there she has stayed. By the time my husband made it back and into hospital to see me he had a son called Dermot and a daughter called Amelia. It seemed fitting, though I never did tell him why I chose Amelia for our daughter's name.

I have always been quite a shy and timid woman. Well, I was. As the mother of twins, I have had to push myself on many occasions. But it is something that I havn't done alone. Amelia has been with me.

She is brave and fierce and encourages me all of the time. When the twins started school, I decided that I wanted to train to be a nurse. My husband wasn't keen, thought that I would be better returning to my previous career in retail. But I dug my heels in, or should I say we did, me and Amelia.

Amelia said that if she could fly across the Atlantic, then I truly could be a mother and a nurse. She was right, I could. And I did.

Amelia Earhart had never had any children of her own and how she delighted in Amelia and Dermot. She encouraged me to encourage them in everything they did.

She is such a positive person. Apart from water, which isn't surprising seeing as she more than likely drowned, but her death is something that we don't talk about. I just remember the first time we went to the beach when the twins were just toddlers, as soon as we began to paddle, I could hear Amelia having some type of panic attack; she was quiet for days after that. Her usual cheer was replaced by melancholy; her word not mine.

So, from then on in, whenever we were going on holiday or to the swimming baths, I would give Amelia warning and she would retreat to wherever it is she goes when she wants some alone time or wants me to.

I have never told anyone about Amelia Earhart, what would you say. She is my secret; well, she was until I saw Joe's forum and made contact with him. It was a relief to know that this wasn't some sort of affliction that had only happened to me.

My husband and I divorced a few years ago and I thought that was that. But fate has a funny way of putting you in the right place at the right time and I met John Rose. I met him here, on 'Who Said That?' We were on the same chat one night and after it ended, I searched him out. We sent messages, then talked on the telephone and eventually he made the journey down from London to here so we could meet in person. And we have been together ever since. Some things are just meant to be, aren't they?

Amelia remains my best friend, my biggest supporter and is as real to me as anyone else in my life.

She is amazing, brave and humble that even after all of this time, people still know who she is.

Why wouldn't we; she was a pioneer for women, their rights and their achievements.

She will never be forgotten, even after I'm gone.

The video ended.

'All these people are so amazing!'

Billy had never thought about how much influence the people in their heads would have on their lives. Billy was learning to play the piano and knew it was something that Freddie Mercury could do, maybe if he let Freddie lead, he would become more accomplished. It was something he would think about. He hadn't had a lesson for months and they didn't have a piano in the house, but his grandma did, maybe they could have it brought over and see if he was better now, he knew about Freddie.

There was no response in his head, so maybe Freddie wasn't as keen on the idea as Billy was.

Chapter 12

'What was that man called? John Rouse? John Rose???'

With that Billy began scrolling through the pages. He could happily have stopped at each one, but he liked to connect to people if he could and Ann Wheeler had a connection, so he would find out all about him!!

Ten minutes later he had found him. And he was off again!

John Rose
London

'Who Said That?' Theodor Seuss Geisel Said That!'

Theodor Seuss Geisel
2nd March 1904 – 24th September 1991
Springfield, Massachusetts, USA
Children's Author, Cartoonist

Hi, I'm John Rose and for anyone who Is not familiar with the name Theodor Geisel, you may know him better as Dr Seuss.

Pretty cool, yes?

This whole 'You Said That?' is pretty new to me. As you can see, I am well into middle age, almost a pensioner. Up until 2 years ago I was just a regular Joe, no dead person's voice in my head or anything.

Then a couple of Christmas's ago I was a famous bookshop in London looking for Christmas presents for my grandchildren. Anyway, as I was looking through the children's book section, this voice says to me 'You must buy them The Grinch that Stole Christmas, it is the most heart-warming of books!'

I looked around and there was no assistant there directing me, there was no one, just a mum and her children sitting at a little table. 'Who Said That?' I thought to myself.

'It's just me, Theo, I know the Grinch that Stole Christmas well and thought seeing as you are buying gifts for your grandchildren that it may be the perfect gift. Obviously, I am extremely biased, and I am somewhat blowing my own trumpet, but no one is blowing it for me so, why not?'

'What do you mean you are blowing your own trumpet?' I thought to myself, I wasn't stupid and knew whatever it was that had spoken to me didn't have a physical presence.

'Oh, I wrote it. My name is Theodor Seuss Geisel, I am Dr Seuss'!

I ignored the voice in my head, found the Grinch that Stole Christmas and a few other books by different authors and left the store.

But I was unnerved all of the way home. On the train home out of London I wracked my brains for a reason why I would suddenly have a voice in my head.

I did not seem to have a temperature, so did not think I was ill. I had not received a bump on the head so was having some sort of concussion episode. I had not eaten anything that I had not eaten before in the past 24 hours so that basically ruled some sort of food poisoning out. There was no reason why all of a sudden, I was hearing voices.

Unless it was something a little more sinister. Perhaps I was getting dementia, that horrible affliction that can affect you when you get old. But I was not really that old, I had not even reached retirement age and I seemed to be managing my job as a mortgage advisor well. In fact, I was doing extremely well in the current climate, making business from the tiniest of leads. But still.

At home I put my shopping away and poured myself a drink.

There was no need to beat myself up, I had simply had an episode and whatever it was had now passed. Maybe the cheese I had ate the night before had been off after all. But the voice had seemed so clear, so concise, and exact that I found it hard to believe that a mouldy piece of cheese could conjure up such a manifestation.

Dr Seuss indeed!!

Nevertheless, for the following weeks I kept a check on what I ate, what I drank, and I made sure that I got plenty of exercise, a walk, a game of squash. And I bought myself a book of puzzles to stretch my mind. If I was going under, I would be doing it fighting.

But there were no more voices. And as Christmas fast approached, I relaxed and looked forward to travelling North to visit my daughter and her family and spend a lovely Christmas and New Year with them.

Packing to leave the day before Christmas Eve, I realised that I had gone way over the top with gifts again. Every year I would begin picking things up on my dinner break in September. A jumper here, a toy there and then I would put them away in a cupboard until it was time to make my journey, then they would all be pulled out, wrapped, and stashed in the boot of my car.

I only hoped that I had enough gift-wrapping paper. They were only a family of four, but you would have thought there was twenty of them if the number of bags in the lounge was anything to go by. Still, it was always great fun wrapping them, putting them into piles by recipient and then placing them into black bin bags ready to go into the car.

I would have myself a glass of wine, nibbles and Christmas Carols sung by crooners from long ago would play in the background.

It had been my Christmas Eve Eve tradition since my daughter had moved to Lincoln and I had travelled up there for the festive period.

I had been on my own for a very long time.

But there were presents to be wrapped and with a glass of wine on the table along with some nice cheese and biscuits, I started on the pile of gifts.

It was taking a very long time. Some of the gifts were so small and fiddly, but they had to all be wrapped so I ploughed on and by the time I was on the last of the bags, it was heading towards midnight. Not ideal when I was setting off early the following morning.

I was just doing the last fold in the wrapping when I heard the voice!

'I am so pleased that you decided to get that for the children! Not because it is one of mine, but because it really does make you feel good!'

I took a peek at what it was I was wrapping. 'The Grinch that Stole Christmas', as if I even needed to look.

'I read it a long time ago, loved it! It has the Who's in it does it not? I liked it because it was about acceptance!'

And then we were chatting. I was finishing off the wrapping and bagging and I was having a conversation with a dead writer in my head.

It was bizarre because he seemed to know Oxford well, which was where I was from, very well. But he had been there he said, studied there. If this voice in my head was a figment of my imagination, it certainly was knowledgeable, how could that even be??

Gifts wrapped and placed in hall ready to be loaded into the car the following morning, I slept badly. Tossed and turned which was not ideal when I had a journey the following day. But the voice had abated, and I eventually got some rest.

And again, all was silent. It maybe was the cheese.

But I was curious. After a wonderful Christmas and New Year, I returned home and began to do some research into what may have happened.

There was little information about voices in your head. Most of the reports I read were written by some strange characters who mainly claimed to be possessed.

I Googled Dr Seuss. True to his word he had been a scholar at Oxford

'Why would I have lied about that??' The voice was back.

Reading through his life, his works and his legacy, I had little choice but to listen as Dr Seuss regaled me with his life story. Clarifying bits, I was reading, speaking of his wives, of the adaptions of the books he had wrote since his death.

And once he was back, this time he did not leave. He was not intrusive. He spoke if he was spoken to.

For a man living on his own, the voice made life a little bit less lonely, though for the life of me I would not have told another soul that I spent my free time mainly talking to myself.

All the while I continued to search for answers. Dr Seuss had no idea how he got there. Just there had been silence and then there had been noise. He was happy to be there though!!

Then I stumbled across 'Who Said That?' and I knew that was where I would maybe find some answers. I did not. What I did find was a number of people who were in the same position as I was, and I found my wife to be!!

Now I do not think I am ill. I still do not know what I am, I just know I am not ill. I am the same as you lot, we are in this together!

The video came to an end. Billy understood what John was saying. Yes, he was still strange himself, but the more videos he watched the more he started to feel normal. That there were people out there that had lived with voices in their heads for years and years. Embraced the voices and continued to live their lives.

Chapter 13

True to his word, Billy continued to share the videos he watched with his mam, his dad and Emily too if they had time. Lockdown restrictions were gently being lifted, everyone was embracing every little bit of freedom they were given and although normality prior to the pandemic still seemed a long way off, it was getting better.

The conservatory was restored to its former glory, with the addition of the piano, which his dad had collected for him and installed into the conservatory before all of the furniture had been put back.

Grandmas and Granddads returned, just into the garden but it was nice that they were all back together and they spent many a day under the newly erected gazebo come rain or shine. It was another new kind of normal.

Billy would be returning to school in September. There would still be no football training or piano lessons, but it would be nice to go to school, something he never thought he would say.

The Government told them to make hay while the sun shone, there was a new scheme coming into force called Eat Out to Help Out, Billy's mam and dad weren't sure about it. But they would order food from local restaurants and eat it under the gazebo!

It was so nice just seeing people that weren't his mam and his dad. Grandmas and Granddads were just as happy to see him and Emily too, and each other. The two couples had been virtually living in isolation for three months.

The decorating business was having a massive boom. The number of businesses that were booking in was blowing my mam and dad's minds, they usually only had a handful of commercial jobs, and their bread and butter were the domestic ones. Now it seemed every business in the North East wanted a facelift.

Whereas the house had been a hive of industry, it was now quiet. Emily was out and about, and Billy would often find himself on his own.

The piano beckoned.

Billy sat on the stool and looked at the keys. He had been having piano lessons with Mrs Brooks for about a year. He was hopeless, he could do a few tunes, badly. But had persevered, mainly because one of his Grandma and Granddad's were paying for the lessons, it had been a Christmas present. Mrs Brooks went to one of his Grandma's clubs and had offered to teach him. But Billy knew that they were wasting their money, he was never going to get it!

Placing his fingers on the keys, he sent a silent message to Freddie Mercury, 'come on then Superstar, make me play'! No answer.

So, Billy played the only thing that he knew by heart. Chop sticks!

Not that having any sheet music at the house would help, he could easily have got the notes up on his phone for something, but he struggled knowing one note from another and relied mainly on where he placed his hands.

Nevertheless, Chop sticks was one that he remembered and tentatively placed his hands on the keys and played it best to his ability. It was rubbish, so he tried it again. And again, and again and eventually it had a tune!

And so, he played it again. Then again. And then again. He knew what he was doing ……

'Enough, enough, I cannot bear it!!' Freddie was there!

'Freddie, you have heard the videos, all the other voices help their bodies. Can you not help me????' Billy asked.

No reply.

'Chop sticks it is then' Billy said out loud.

Despite playing it at least a dozen times. There was nothing. No shouts of protest, just nothing!

Chapter 14

Giving it up Billy made his way upstairs and decided he would go and watch a couple of videos. There were so many of them and if he sat from then until Christmas, he probably wouldn't have been able to watch every single one.

But one or two for now wouldn't hurt!

Randomly he clicked on a face!

Phil Johnson
Margate

'Who Said That? Thomas Parker Said That!'

Thomas Parker
22nd December 1843 – 5th December 1915
Coalbrookdale, England
Electric Car Pioneer

Legacy
Lead-acid Battery, Electric Tram, Electric Car, smokeless fuel

Interesting Billy thought to himself. There was so much talk about people changing to electric cars these day, like it was a new thing. But his bloke died in 1915, over 100 years ago!

Pressing the video, Billy lay back on his bed to see what Phil Johnson had to say about the inventor of the electric car!

Hello, I'm Phil and I have always had Thomas Parker in my head.

I think I was born with him!

It made me strange, still does. I bet you all have really famous people, household names.

Even if I told people about Thomas, no one would know who he was. I didn't. It took me years to find out who he was. I had him long before you could Google someone and read all about them on Wikipedia. I had to go to the library and hunt through books and books using snippets of information that Thomas gave me.

But back when I was young I was frightened of Thomas. Not of the voice in my head, I had no notion that everyone did not have such a thing, but he was quite a stern man and when I acted up, he made it very clear that such behaviour would not be tolerated. So not only was strange, but I was also strange, strange. Incredibly well behaved for a little boy. So much so that my mum, dad and teachers thought that there was something wrong with me. I told my mum, dad and teachers about the voice in my head, but they dismissed it as fantasy and told me not to talk rubbish. I stopped talking about Thomas at that point.

I excelled at school even when I was quite young, especially at the sciences, obviously all thanks to Thomas Parker.

And I realised that not everyone had a voice in their head. In fact, no one did. So, I was either really special, or there was something wrong with me. Either way the voice stayed and as I got older, we talked.

What a great man Thomas Parker is. He is just so clever. The progress he made with electricity is mind blowing. But of all of the things that he has invented, the electric car is the one that blows my mind.

At that point I think Thomas gave little thought to Climate Change, he was around in the midst of the industrial revolution, when everything was burnt and dug and they gave little thought to the damage that they were doing to the planet. Thomas Parker invented the electric car because he could, he was that clever.

By the time I was in my teens, Thomas's influence had rubbed off on me. We talked about my schoolwork, about how science had changed and what I was learning at school. I was passionate about physics and biology, and I loved chemistry.

So much so that by the time I left school I had decided that I wanted to be a doctor.

Dr Phillip Johnson; that's me!

I have a wife and family now. My wife is ironically a psychologist, I met her at Medical School. She knows all about Thomas Parker, is as stumped as I have always been as to why he is with me. It was my wife that actually found 'Who Said That?', she is forever looking for answers, but beyond her, no one knows about Thomas Parker. I am still as strange as ever.

Thomas and I still talk. He is amazed with the world, the inventions and the improvements to things that were around in his day at the turn of the century.

He is a pretty awesome companion to have. Remember the name, Thomas Parker, inventor!

Billy was once again blown away. How could he have invented an electric car all of those years ago? Everyone was banging on about them these days, but no one had ever mentioned Thomas Parker. Billy thought it had been Tesla!! Who knew??

Chapter 15

Next to Phil Johnson, or Dr Phillip Johnson was a member who looked about the same age as Billy.

'Let's see what you have going on!!' Billy said to himself seeing as Freddie Mercury remained silent in his head.

George Harris
Stockton on Tees

'Who Said That? Charlie Chaplin Said That?

Sir Charles Spencer Chaplin Junior
16th April 1889 – 25th December 1977
London England
Actor, Comedian

Legacy
Time Magazine Top 100 Most Important People of the 20th Century
10th Greatest Male Star of Classic Hollywood Cinema
Top 10 Directors of All Time
Chaplin's World Museum
Tramp Statue in London
9 Blue Plaques
Hollywood Walk of Fame
Knight Commander of the Order of the British Empire

3 Academy Awards
Academy Awards Honorary Award
Fellow of the British Academy of Film and Television Arts
6 Films preserved in the National Film Registry by the United States Library of Congress

George didn't live too far away from Billy. It made Billy feel better. The whole Freddie Mercury thing in his head had come as a bit of a shock if he was honest. It made him think that if there hadn't been the lockdown and his Granddad's box of DVD's would he had forgotten all about Freddie Mercury, or was he there all of the time just waiting for the right moment? He would never know; Freddie was there and just like all of the people's videos he had watched so far on the 'Who Said That?' Forum, he was just going to have to live with it. But knowing that George Harris wasn't far away and had a dead person in his head too, made him feel better. That was two on the 'Who Said That? Forum who lived within spitting distance of him!

Billy fired off a message to George telling him that he lived in North East too and did he fancy a chat?

Then he pressed play on George's video and sat back on his bed to listen to see how Charlie Chaplin had got into George's head.

I'm George Harris and I have Charlie Chaplin's voice in my head.

Charlie must have always been there, but I can't remember him from when I was little. My mam said that I used to do his walk though. You know with toes pointing outwards and legs together. How could I have known to do that if he hadn't already been in my head?

Oh, and I used to have conversations with myself. My mam thought it was because I was an only child. So, he must have always been there.

My first memory, if you can call it that was at school. We were having a show for the 'end of the year', and I been selected to host it. I was terrified. I hadn't volunteered to do anything when the parts came out. But as teachers do when you don't want them to, the ones that don't want to do anything get the big parts.

I was really scared. I didn't want to stand up in front of my wholes class, worse still whole school and all the teachers and the parents.

On the first day we were rehearsing I was shaking un my shoes. I would be first up and then every bit in between. It was all too much!

I had a script to read, I would be able to keep it with me during performances the teacher said, and she said I should relax and just be me!

And then that was the first time I heard the voice properly in my head.

'Why would you want to be you when you can be someone else. Even when you are being you there is no reason you cannot also be someone else!'

I knew it was in my head. I had heard the voice before, many times, but that was the first time I could remember it talking to me directly.

'What do you mean?' I asked back, in my head of course.

'Well, I always find that facial expressions can go a long way. A raise of the eyebrow here, a scowl, your face can tell a million stories. And make people laugh. It is good to make people laugh. Should we give this a go, together!'

That was when I became a comedian.

I still had no idea whose voice it was. But as we started the rehearsals, I had my own personal director in my head. He was good. He was very good.

By opening night, I knew I could do it. I could read off the script if I needed to, but somehow, I knew I wouldn't need to. Within minutes I had people laughing out loud, but just like the voice had said, a facial expression could do the work for you.

I blew everyone away. Shy, timid, quiet George was a dark horse!

But I knew it had been the voice much more than it was ever me. If it had been up to me, I would have pretended I was ill and not done it at all. The voice was giving me an ever-growing confidence in myself.

And I still had no idea what his name was even.

'Thank you' I said to myself!

'I am just pleased your show was a success. I could hear the raucous laughter.' The voice replied.

'What is your name??' I asked.

'Charles, well Charlie. Charlie Chaplin!' Charlie answered.

'Like THE Charlie Chaplin' I screamed

'Yes, I suppose I am, The Tramp, the one with the funny walk!'

I could not believe it. The voice was Charlie Chaplin. It was something that Charlie found very funny. He was famous for not having a voice, the majority of his films were silent, no wonder he was so good at explaining facial……

VIDEO CHAT!

It was George Harris!!

Billy answered the call and George took up the screen.

'Hi Billy, pleased you got in touch. You aren't far away from me at all are you??'

Billy was surprised how much older George looked in comparison to his membership picture and his video.

They chatted for the next hour.

George was 18 now, the video was made 3 years ago when he was about Billy's age. He was blown away with Freddie Mercury, again Billy felt Freddie shake his inner peacock feathers, he was there, listening!

But Billy was equally impressed with Charlie Chaplin. He was a legend and even though Billy had never seen a single one of his films, he was still an iconic character and would have known him anywhere. George said Charlie said thank you. It was surreal, Billy Watson from Newcastle was talking to Charlie Chaplin, in a fashion anyway.

George was at drama school, well he had been before the pandemic, but hoped that he would be able to return in September. After the initial school thing, George had taken a liking to being centre stage, he had no idea how that had happened he had said laughing.

Because Billy hadn't quite finished George's video, George filled him in.

After they had sorted who he was, George had looked up everything that he could possibly find out about him. He said he became a little bit obsessed with him, watched the films, read all the biographies and autobiographies. He had even been to visit his statue in London.

George said that it wasn't so much the voice in his head, he was just fascinated with how a very poor boy from London could become so famous. It was a good story.

He said Charlie was a constant in his life. They spoke most days and he was very good at directing George when he had auditions and such.

They were friends.

Billy told him all about Freddie Mercury, how he like George seemed to have always had him, he told George to watch his 'Who Said That?' video and see what had happened when he was four years old.

But unlike George's Charlie Chaplin, Freddie didn't seem to want to do anything for Billy.

The boys agreed that once all of the restrictions were lifted it would be good to meet up and talk, George drove so he could even come to Billy's house if that was ok with his parents.

Billy liked George, he hoped that he could make a good career out of acting.

Call over, Billy switched off his laptop and wandered downstairs to see what was happening, he could smell food so his mam must be home and he wanted to tell her about George and the other video he had watched.

Chapter 16

Billy was right, his mam was cooking.

It was a nice night, so the Grandmas and Granddads and Emily's boyfriend were all there to eat in the garden.

Not wanting to be given a job off his mam, Billy went to say hi to everyone in the garden, the Downing Street Press Conference had just been on, and everyone was talking animatedly about the hope for some more restrictions being lifted. It was mad, they were all in the garden and still they sat as far away from each other as they could. Billy's dad had even opened up the garage door so their guests could use the loo without going through the house. The sooner normality returned the better.

Billy wandered back into the kitchen for a drink, but this time instead of going into the garden he went to the conservatory and sat on the stool in front of the piano.

Chop sticks it is, he thought placing his hands above the appropriate keys.

As Billy went to hit the first key, his hand flew over and started hitting a different set of keys!!

'You have guilt tripped me quite enough now, all those do Gooding voices; I could not sit through another. I am not the best pianist, but I can play a tune; especially one I know well. So, relax and let me guide you! Let us have some fun! Let's be friends like the other voices are!'

With that, Billy lost control of his hands and fingers. But the tune was recognisable straight away!

Under Pressure!!

Billy watched his hands mesmerised as they flew over the keys and Freddie Mercury sang in his head.

It finished and Billy sneaked a look out the conservatory door. The whole family were watching him. But he had no time to say anything because no sooner had they finished then Freddie took control again!

We Are the Champions

Then Killer Queen, Don't Stop Me Now, I Want to Break Free!!!

Billy played on and on. Note perfect. With the still singing Freddie Mercury in his head.

By the time he had finished A Kind of Magic, he was exhausted and so must have been Freddie.

'I think that may be enough for one day don't you think?? But I have enjoyed myself, I just don't have enough in me for Bohemian Rhapsody, but maybe tomorrow!'

'Thanks Freddie, you are amazing. The greatest!'

Then Billy knew that Freddie had retreated to whatever corner of Billy's mind he went to when he wanted some alone time.

Billy put down the lid of the piano and made his way outside. He was starving.

They were all staring at him as if he was an alien. Not just them though, both the next-door neighbours and their children were hanging over the hedge; they had been listening. Billy thought maybe the whole street had heard, it had been quite loud.

'Thank God for Lockdown!' his mam said. 'Billy has been practising so hard, looks like all that hard work has paid off!"

Everyone started to clap. Billy felt a bit of a fraud but took the applause anyway. And somewhere in his mind he could feel Freddie's peacock feathers rustling.

'Yes Freddie, that is for you. No one has forgotten about you!!'

But there was no response.

Billy caught Emily's eye, she was smiling at him, which didn't always happen, after all they were brother and sister, and it was more often than not a scowl he got, or she ignored him altogether! But she actually looked like she was proud of him for embracing his inner Freddie.

Billy just hoped that they didn't ask for an encore anytime soon. Freddie was lost to him; for the time being anyway.

They didn't. Emily brought out a speaker and stuck a playlist on and although the grandmas and granddads asked him lots of questions about how he had got so good, no one asked him to play again.

Chapter 17

And that was probably the day that Billy Watson and Freddie Mercury bonded.

Freddie seemed to be more relaxed the more they played together. Billy became more proficient on the piano, he could even just about manage to play the pieces that Mrs Brooks, his piano teacher had sent him.

Even though Freddie insisted that he wasn't very good, Billy disagreed. It wasn't just Queen music they played, they played Elton John, the Beatles, and other songs that Billy had heard but had no idea who had sung them. And all just using Freddie's memory.

The house was full of music.

Restrictions continued to be lifted, for the meantime anyway, the talk was all of the re-introduction of lockdowns in the winter, but who knew!

Billy still went on the Zoom Chats on the 'Who Said That?' Forum. Every week there seemed to be a new member, there must have been almost 500 members altogether, all mashed up so it had been decided that they would all pay a subscription fee and upgrade the forum easier to navigate.

George had offered to help organise and the first person he had asked to help him was Billy. It would be a massive job, every member would have to be categorised, but even before that they would have to decide what the categories would be. But Billy was happy to help.

Football still wasn't back on, and his piano lessons were given using a sheet of music sent to him via email which Mrs Brooks sent to him religiously even though she had no idea what progress Billy was making.

School would be returning, but not every day, it was going to be a phased return, so as Summer came to an end, Billy would have more than enough time to sit and watch the videos on the 'Who Said That? Forum.

Opening the shared spreadsheet that had been set up to record each member, Billy was surprised to see that there were a couple already in there, including himself.

Billy Watson	Newcastle	From Birth	Freddie Mercury	Musician
George Harris	Stockton	From Birth	Charlie Chaplin	Actor

Clicking On the first member on the page, Billy noted down.

Nicola McNeil
Glasgow

'Who Said That?? Elvis Presley Said That!'

Elvis Aaron Presley
8th January 1935 – 16th August 1977
Tupelo, Mississippi, USA
Singer. Actor

Legacy
Guinness Book of Records Best Selling Solo Music Artist
500 – 1 billion sales
Most Gold Albums
25 Multi-Platinum Albums
33 Movies

Billy coped the information on onto the next line of the spreadsheet.

Billy Watson	Newcastle	From Birth	Freddie Mercury	Musician
George Harris	Stockton	From Birth	Charlie Chaplin	
Actor				
Nicola McNeil	Glasgow	?	Elvis Presley	
Musician				

Returning to the 'Who Said That? Forum, Billy pressed play on the video and he was off!

Hello All, My name is Nichola ....

Billy settled back onto his bed and watched to see what Nicola and her famous dead person was all about!

'Who is the voice???' Freddie was there, he always seemed to be there when Billy was on the 'Who Said That?' Forum. 'Did I hear correctly; did I hear Elvis??'

'Yes, Freddie. She said she had Elvis Presley!! Did you know him??'

'No, no. But I would like to…. 'Freddie had a pleading tone to his voice!

'Let's just see what the video is all about and then we will see what happens!'

But Billy doubted Freddie had heard him, he was doing his own rendition of some old Elvis song, loudly.

Billy paused the video and waited for Freddie to finish. As often happened these days… it was all about Freddie Mercury!!!

A Note From the Author

I hope that you enjoyed reading Who Said That?? as much as I liked writing it.

It's something different. And I learned so much!!

And if you did like it; please spread the word; it is so difficult getting books out to the masses when you do it all yourself.

But I have a head full of stories so check out the ones already written and keep an eye out for news ones.

Love Gill xxx

Printed in Great Britain
by Amazon